Mama Wrex

Written and Illustrated by
Rebekah Major

This story is dedicated to my mama, Kristine,
who is always there for me and whom I love very much!

Mama Wrex

Written and Illustrated
by Rebekah Major
Book design by Tara Sizemore
Published August 2014
Little Creek Books
Imprint of Jan-Carol Publishing, Inc

ISBN: 978-1-939289-46-9
Library of Congress Control Number: 2014947672

You may contact the publisher:
Jan-Carol Publishing, Inc
PO Box 701
Johnson City, TN 37605
Email: publisher@jancarolpublishing.com
Website: jancarolpublishing.com

Jan-Carol
Publishing, Inc
"every story needs a book"

Dear Reader,

Every year at Christmas, my father gives my brother and me each a beautifully wrapped gift. When the gift is opened, it seems to contain only tissue. But this gift is the best of all the gifts under the tree–it is the gift of love!
This story of unconditional love comes from my heart and is my gift of love to all who read it.
–Rebekah

"Love is patient and kind; love does not envy or boast; it is not arrogant or rude.
It does not insist on its own way; it is not irritable or resentful;
it does not rejoice at wrongdoing, but rejoices with the truth.
Love bears all things, believes all things, hopes all things, endures all things."
Corinthians 13:4-7

Acknowledgments

I thank my father, Robert, and his wife, Gail, for never allowing me to forget my passions, talents, and dreams.
This book would not have been possible without you!

You may find it hard to ignore
that my Mama's a T-Rex dinosaur.

I like to splash in the tub,
but bath time ended with a giant thud.

Look at all the milk on the floor!
But Mama Wrex I still adore.

T.Rexadore
bek

It’s hard to keep yourself composed
when you’re wearing hole-y clothes.

Clean
yes
Shine

I try not to be gloomy and fuss,
when Mama Wrex eats my school bus.

STOP
SCHOOL BUS

I try to explain to my teacher
my Mama Wrex's distinctive feature,
which made my homework–I greatly fear–
to completely disappear!

You're Dino-Mite!
home work due today!
7 + 3 =
11 + 5 =
12 + 4 =
5 + 20 =
Home work
Hang in there
TRi your best!

Fishing is not much competition
when Mama wants a belly addition.

My sandcastle walls tumble and crumble
when Mama has a great big stumble.

When my Mama prances and dances,
I want to hide wherever France is.

My Mama Wrex's kite
never quite took flight
after one enormous bite.

B

When Mama splashed me with a puddle,
I didn't get to scoot or scuttle.

The moon and stars shine bright at night
at our lovely camping site.
We cook our marshmallows on the fire.
Her love for me will never tire.

During the glory of story time,
the action freezes at page nine.
Because my Mama ate page ten,
we have to buy that book again.

TORY
of the
Loud
and
We

I lay in bed and count some sheep,
trying hard to fall asleep.
In my mind they do take flight,
but Mama catches them at night.

I love my Mama with all my might,
and now it's time to say "Good night!"

CPSIA information can be obtained at www.ICGtesting.com
Printed in the USA
BVOW11s2058170914
367330BV00002B/2/P

9 781939 289469